NOTHING-IMPOSSIBLE-POSSUM™ STORIES

by

Marjorie Ainsborough Decker

Illustrated by

Colleen Murphy Scott

A Faith Adventure Book
from **CHRISTIAN MOTHER GOOSE**™

Back Cover Photo by Dave Canaday

CHRISTIAN MOTHER GOOSE™ WORLD
Grand Junction, Colorado   81502

NOTHING-IMPOSSIBLE-POSSUM™ STORIES

CHRISTIAN MOTHER GOOSE™

Un Petit Enfant Les Conduira ™

#1 National Bestseller Author
MARJORIE AINSBOROUGH DECKER

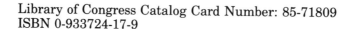

is well-known and loved for her distinct story-telling style. Her CHRISTIAN MOTHER GOOSE™ CLASSICS have endeared the trust of parents and the twinkle of children across the world.

Library of Congress Catalog Card Number: 85-71809
ISBN 0-933724-17-9

Printed in the United States of America.
First Edition   July 1985
Second Edition   November 1985

"Friends! Welcome to my 'NOTHING-IMPOSSIBLE-POSSUM'™ STORIES! CHRISTIAN MOTHER GOOSE™ and I want to share some very special secrets with you ... And some very special places where only your faith can take you! I know you can! ..."

Your Friend Always..
"Nip"

CONTENTS

Today, the charming characters from the growing WORLD OF CHRISTIAN MOTHER GOOSE™ are inspiring families throughout the land with Bestselling books, quality music and audio products, fine gifts, activity programs, video, and now licensed doll and plush toy collectibles.

THE UN-TANGLING CAN

To begin a fine day
In the finest of way,
There is nothing much handier than
A smooth-soothe-out device,
To keep everything nice;
Yes, I have one! An Un-Tangling Can!

Now an Un-Tangling Can
Has a spout that can span
All the way from right here to up there!
So the tangles you meet,
In your house, field or street,
Can be fixed and smoothed out anywhere!

In my can is a balm,
With a perfume to calm
Any squabble or tangled-up mess;
And its rich, creamy oil
In a flash can uncoil
Twisted tangles, with ease and success!

6

I can untangle horns,
Even those with sharp thorns,
And I untangle them in quick style;
I can untangle rope,
Tied in knots without hope,
And rewind it in neatly stacked pile!

When my pal, Porcupine,
Wore a coat made of twine,
And then found he could not get undressed;
He just called for the man
With the Un-Tangling Can,
To unravel his problem's request!

When a rabbit named Jack,
Thought he'd mastered the knack
Of the high-jump across a tall fence;
But one day missed his mark,
And got stuck in the bark,
I retrieved him with little expense!

Once, the Weasel twins tried
To get both heads inside
Of a tempting, half-full stewing pan;
When they couldn't get out,
I just popped in a spout
Full of oil from my Un-Tangling Can!

I am glad to report,
Twisted words, long and short,
Have untangled, and calmly smoothed out
In a wonderful way,
As I gave them a spray
Through my Un-Tangling Can's friendly spout!

So with horns and with thorns,
And with rope without hope,
And with rabbits with habits that stick;
With stuck-tight weasel twins,
And with porcupines' pins,
They can all be untangled, so quick!
But with words you have heard
That have hurt, be alert!
Be determined to stand like a man!
Till they're all straightened out
With the oil from the spout
Of your very own Un-Tangling Can!

8

NOTHING IS IMPOSSIBLE WITH GOD!

Nothing is impossible,
Nothing is impossible,
Nothing is impossible with God!

On the one hand there's the seed;
   On the other, there's the tree!
In between is God to do
   What's impossible for me!

On the one hand there's the hill;
   On the other, there's the way!
In between is God to do
   What isn't possible, they say!

On the one hand there's the tear;
   On the other, there's the song;
In between is God to right
   The most impossible wrong!

On the one hand there's the boy;
   On the other, there's the king!
In between is God to do
   The most impossible thing!

Nothing is impossible,
Nothing is impossible,
Nothing is impossible with God!

TO FLY OR NOT TO FLY?

Poor Benjamin Bumblebee,
They said he couldn't fly;
"He's much too roly-poly
To lift into the sky.
Hopping might just fit him;
He might learn by-and-by
To jump into the air — but,
He'll never, never fly!"

Poor Benjamin Bumblebee,
Would make no quick reply,
But whispered down inside him,
"As God made me, so am I!
See here — He gave me wings;
And wings fly! — I can't deny;
My roly-poly bumble
On my wings it must rely."

While everyone still argued
The pro's and con's of why,
"Poor Benjamin will never,
Oh! never reach the sky,"
Benjamin buzzed his wings,
Shouting loudly, *"Yes, I'll try!"*
Straight off he flew his roly-
Poly bumble to the sky!

10

BARNACLE BEN AND BARNACLE BESS

Nothing-Impossible-Possum one day,
    Found two crusty barnacles sunk in dismay.
They sat all alone on the River Dee sand,
    Shaking their heads, as they sat hand-in-hand.

"What can I do for you, as a new friend?
    You look as if everything reached a sad end.
I'm Nothing-Impossible-Possum," said 'NIP',
    "I gather you're waiting to catch the next ship?"

"I'm Barnacle Ben; she's my Barnacle Bess;
    The reason we sit here in this deep distress
Is, we've been dislodged from the ship that we ride;
    It's cruel and heartless to be cast aside."

"What kind of a job did you have on that ship?"
    Asked Nothing-Impossible-Possum, (or 'NIP');
"What kind of a job? They are words to lament!"
    Said Barnacle Ben. "We just *rode* where it went."

11

"We clung to the bottom, without any fuss;
   We never made trouble; no one noticed us;
We have no ambition for so-called success;
   We went where the ship went," said Barnacle Bess.

"That's true," said her partner, old Barnacle Ben,
  "We rode anywhere that it took us, and then
We never complained if it went east or west,
   But trusted the ship to do what it does best."

"You've made no decisions at all in your life!
   Concerning direction for you and your wife?
My, my this is time for this positive NIP,
   To get you to think other things than a ship!"

"A barnacle riding won't gather much moss;
   There must be a way you can be your own boss;
It's never too late, Ben, to get a new grip,"
   Said Nothing-Impossible-Possum, (or 'NIP').

"You think at *our* age, we can get a new grip
   On more than the bottom of some moving ship?
I tremble to think of the strain and the stress
   Such change would impose on my Barnacle Bess!"

"Dear Barnacle Ben, this is time to confess
   My feelings were hurt," said his Barnacle Bess;
The day they dislodged us, I heard the ship's mate
   Say you and I both were a crusty dead-weight!"

"*Now*! That makes a difference," said Barnacle Ben;
  "Dead-weight, did they say? Well, we'll not ride again
On any such thing as an ungrateful ship;
  I've made up my mind. We *will* get a new grip!"

"To make up your mind, that's the first step to do,
  To start a new life full of challenge for you!
A positive barnacle soon can equip
  His dreams," said the Nothing-Impossible-NIP.

"Our dreams, did you say?" whispered Barnacle Bess,
  "For years, as we drifted, I had to suppress
A deep, hidden longing that plagued me inside:
  'How nice to buy tickets, and *choose* where to ride'."

"Then here is Step Two, to that dream's satisfaction;
  We'll back up Step One with some definite action!
I know that the lighthouse on Cockle-Bay strip,
  Is looking for help," said the positive NIP.

"I do believe, dear, this has worked out for good,"
  Said Barnacle Ben, and Bess quite understood.
"Then off to the lighthouse I'll guide you," said NIP,
  "And this will be different than riding a ship!"

13

So, Barnacle Ben with his Barnacle Bess,
 Held hands as they walked in a new hopefulness.
At first, they were fearful to choose their own way,
 But NIP kept encouraging them to the Bay.

The old lighthouse keeper said, "Fortunate me!
 A barnacle has much experience at sea,
And knows all the ways of a sea-faring ship;
 What fine lighthouse keepers they'll make, Mr. NIP!"

And now when you see Cockle-Bay's light at night,
 It's Barnacle Ben who earns keep, keeping light!
Instead of just clinging below on a trip,
 It's Barnacle Ben who's now guiding the ship!

And Barnacle Bess? Well, her dream *did* come true;
 They now buy a ticket, and cruise with a view!
They've even sent gifts to the town's Sharing Ship;
 Three cheers for the Nothing-Impossible-NIP!

GROWING!

I'm just a little tortoise;
    Slow . . . slow . . . slow .
But I *do* have places to
    Go . . . go . . . go .
You ask me how I'll go there? I'll
    Show . . show . . . show .
One step at a time on each
    Tip . . . tip . . . toe!

I'm just a little fellow,
    Slow . . . slow . . . slow .
But to be like Jesus, I'll
    Grow . . . grow . . . grow .
You ask me how I'll grow so? I'll
    Show . . . show . . . show .
One step at a time on each
    Tip . . . tip . . . toe!

UPSTREAM, DOWNSTREAM

The sun was tip-toeing over the top of the Mustard Mountains as Nothing-Impossible-Possum stopped along the river bank to examine a Compass Plant.

Travelers in the Mustard Mountains find the Compass Plant a friendly guide. Its upper leaves always point north and south the minute they are touched by sunshine.

"Yes, I'm going in the right direction," said Nothing-Impossible-Possum to his very own self.

"Follow this river bank upstream, keep going north, and then I should reach the Crystal Caves."

Thinking of the Crystal Caves and what they might hold, made him happy. And as he had just reached a steep hill, it was an especially good time to think happy thoughts.

Climbing up the hill, he sang a song between huffs and puffs. He made it up as he went along:

"Upstream, upstream,
Yes! we're going upstream;
Never fear, we'll get there!
Yes! we're going upstream!"

Nothing-Impossible-Possum liked the sound of the new song, and only had to sing it five times before he reached the top of the hill.

16

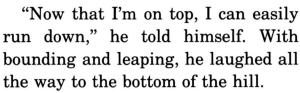

"Now that I'm on top, I can easily run down," he told himself. With bounding and leaping, he laughed all the way to the bottom of the hill.

His knapsack of food bumped up and down on his back as he ran. "Breakfast, breakfast, now it's time for breakfast," it seemed to say as it thumped and bumped.

"Thank you for reminding me, knapsack. And here's a nice grassy spot waiting for me to set a table."

Nothing-Impossible-Possum is fond of sitting at a table to eat, so the first thing he unpacked from the knapsack was a little linen cloth. When he spread it out on the grass, he had his own table in an instant. Four smooth rocks were handy to hold down each corner.

As he unpacked apples, mushrooms, nuts and brown bread, he began another song:

"He prepares a table for me,
A table for me,
A table for me;
He prepares a table for me
Up in the Mustard Mountains."

17

"Not a table, not a table, not a table," the gurgling river seemed to shout as it rushed by.

"Not a table! Of course this is a table," the little possum shouted back.

"Has no legs, has no legs, has no legs," the river gurgled on.

It's not the *legs* that make a table. It's the *top* that counts. Four legs without a top? Now that is *not* a table; but a *top* without legs — that *still* can be a table." Not worrying about the river's remarks anymore, Nothing-Impossible-Possum went back to his singing.

By now, the sun was very warm, and strolling brightly across the Mustard Mountains.

"It's a good time for breakfast," the cheerful traveler decided, and closed his eyes to pray.

"Plop, swish! Plop, swish!" The sound of a rowing paddle made him look up as soon as he had said, "Amen."

Paddling hard upstream came Cobblecut the cobbler; the smallest of the five cobblers who live at the foot of Mustard Mountains.

Cobblecut spied the white cloth right away, and pulled over to the bank.

"Good morning, Nip," he shouted.

(Nothing - Impossible - Possum doesn't mind at all being called "Nip" by his friends.)

"Hello, there, Cobblecut! Come and join me for breakfast, and tell me where you're off to."

Cobblecut got out of the log canoe and sat down at the legless table. "I'm on my way to Timberwind with tools and leather. They want to start a cobbler's 'Good News' shoe shop up there, and I'm going to teach them the trade."

The little cobbler and possum talked of good things as they shared breakfast together in the warm sunshine.

As they finished, Cobblecut asked, "Now . . . where are you going, Nip?"

"I'm going up to the Crystal Caves to look for relics of the Tool-makers and the Tale-makers. They lived on these mountains many years ago, and I hear the Crystal Caves hold some of their secrets."

"Well, without a doubt, Nothing-Impossible-Possum is the very one to find such things," said Cobblecut, with a twinkle in his eye. "I'd be happy to give you a ride upstream, and save you some walking. The Crystal Caves are close to Timberwind."

"Thank you, Cobblecut. I'll help you paddle up the river."

So without any more delay, Possum folded his cloth back into the knapsack.

Cobblecut took his place in the front of the boat. "You make yourself comfortable in the back, Nip," he said. The bags of tools and leather filled the rest of the canoe.

"Plop, swish! Plop, swish!" They were soon paddling upstream and enjoying the sound of the paddles as they pushed along.

"It's not easy going upstream," Cobblecut observed. "I'm glad that you're here to help."

Suddenly, a blue jay screeching in the sky caught their attention. "Danger, danger! The river is flooding!" the blue jay kept shrieking.

"Hold on, Cobblecut!" shouted Nothing-Impossible-Possum, as rushing waters tumbled around the bend. How frightening it was as the river raced down to engulf the little log canoe. It was all the struggling friends could do to hold on to their paddles.

This way and that way, the boat was tossed, but Cobblecut and Nip pushed as hard as they could against the strong waves.

Then from the back of the heaving canoe Nothing-Impossible-Possum began to sing:

"Upstream, upstream,
Yes! we're going upstream!
Never fear, we'll get there;
Yes! we're going upstream!"

He shouted louder as the waters crashed against them, "Sing, Cobblecut! This is the song of the hour!"

And between gulps of river water getting in their mouths, and paddling hard to keep their canoe pointed upstream, they kept on singing, "Upstream, upstream, Yes! we're going upstream!"

No sooner had Possum said those words when another great surge of water raced down upon them. It was filled with little rafts and logs bobbing down with the rushing waves.

All sorts of little creatures were holding on to the rafts. They shouted as they sailed passed the brave log canoe:

"Downstream, downstream,
Yes! we're going downstream;
On we go, with the flow,
Easy-sailing downstream!"

"Upstream, upstream!" two voices kept on singing, as four small arms kept pushing with all their might against the swirling river.

Struggling to keep his place in the canoe, Nothing-Impossible-Possum's mind remembered what he had learned from a Tale-maker's story Grandpa Mole had told him... "When you pass through the waters, I will be with you; and through the rivers, they shall not overflow you..." Oh, what courage those words gave him! And what added strength!

"Upstream, upstream,
Yes! we're going upstream!
Thank You, Lord,
You're aboard,
Yes! we're going upstream!"

21

Cobblecut caught the new words right away, and took extra courage, too, as he sang along.

And through it all, the little log canoe kept her nose pointed upstream!

Right then, huge wings swept above them. It was Christian Mother Goose!

She landed on a bank nearby and called across the river, "Keep on keeping on! The waters are slowing down ahead of you. It was a flash flood. The worst is over. Bravo! You'll soon reach your goal!" Then off she flew again.

At the sound of those cheering words, the Beaver family popped up out of the waters. They cheered the little boat, too, as it still struggled on.

The big waves soon began to sink lower and lower. Cobblecut and Nothing-Impossible-Possum were now too tired to sing anymore. But their paddles went "Plop, swish! Plop, swish!" again as they reached kinder waters.

At last they came in sight of the Crystal Caves. They felt like heroes; soaking wet; with arms that ached; but the knapsack and bags of tools and leather were still safe in the canoe.

"Let's lie down on the bank to dry out and take a rest," sighed Cobblecut, as they moored the canoe.

"I can't wait," agreed Nip.

Stretched out on the grassy bank, the two little friends soon fell fast asleep. Cobblecut snored. Nothing-Impossible-Possum kept murmuring in his sleep,"Upstream, upstream. Yes! we're going upstream!" as he dreamed of what he would find in the Crystal Caves . . .

But that's another story!

THE BUSHEL BASKET BUILDERS

Hear, lads and lassies!
This story abounds
With curious bushel
Baskets around.

This particular kind
Of basket is made
To keep little lights
Hidden off in the shade!

Hundreds of candles,
With soft, little lights,
Go into these baskets,
To keep out of sight!

The builders of such
Bushel baskets reside
On this side and that side
Of land, sea and tide.

It's a popular trade,
With some veneration;
Fine bushels you'll find
All over creation!

The Mackintosh clan
In the hills of Loch-Lad,
Built their bushel basket
Of red and green plaid!

The Zyder-Zee folk,
    In a large tulip crop,
Built their bushel basket
    With a windmill on top!

Far out in the West,
    Where the mountains are found,
They build bushel baskets
    With roofs to the ground!

The Falls of Niagara
    Find most opportune
The waterproof kind,
    On a floating pontoon!

Even the desert
    Has not been exempt,
And their bushel baskets
    Are made like striped tents!

And up in the North,
    They are fond of a wall
To circle their bushels,
    So they're not seen at all!

Some bushel baskets
    Are centuries old!
Faithfully keeping
    Light hidden, I'm told!

And, oh! they are keeping
    Their light hidden well;
For none has been seen
    Shining through their thick shell!

25

But out in the fields;
   Running down every street,
Are happy light-holders,
   On light, skipping feet!

They've never made bushels;
   (They *do* make a noise!)
They're loved everywhere as:
   "Those dear girls and boys!"

They carry a candle
   With cheery-lit wick
Carefully placed on
   A nice candlestick!

Lighting up pathways,
   And lighting up stairs;
Uptown, or downtown,
   A candlestick's there!

So while bushel baskets
   Stand off in the dark,
The children are spreading
   The light, spark by spark!

Hurrah! For the children!
   They've made no designs
To make bushel baskets;
   Hurrah! Their light shines!

EBENEZER EAGLE'S WART

Ebenezer Eagle woke up feeling very sad. A wart had been growing on his beak for some time, and now he could no longer ignore it.

And more alarming still, he was sure the wart was the reason for some strange things that had been happening to him lately.

When he tried to land on a high, narrow ledge in the cliffs, he kept missing the mark and losing his balance. This was cause for great concern to an eagle who could see a speck a mile away, and swoop down upon that speck in a flash, because he knew it was really a tasty bit of dinner.

As Ebenezer thought about his amazing flying feats, it brought back memories of wonderful days.

"I have expert balance; and I'm more graceful than a trapeze artist at flying, swooping and gliding high," he comforted himself. "Well, I *used* to be an expert at that sort of thing," he slowly admitted to himself.

His head drooped forlornly. "Miles into the air with freedom and power . . . that was you . . . yes, *you*, Ebenezer Eagle. Riding high above the storms whenever you wanted to. Oh, they were glorious days . . . I wonder if they are over?"

He raised his head to look up in the sky; "King of birds, that's what they called me. It really was a very nice title to own."

"I wonder if anyone else has noticed my clumsiness? In all my years it never once crossed my mind that I would get into such an awkward state. There must be something wrong; and the only 'something' that I can see is this wart on my beak."

Ebenezer then looked over the edge of his cliff home. For the first time since he was a very little eaglet, he felt frightened, and timid. The valley *did* look so very far down below.

"I don't think I will try any difficult flights today. But now that I think about it, it never used to be difficult to land on a thin strip of rock overhanging the cliffs. Yet I've missed that ledge for weeks, and wobbled off a number of times. Where has my balance gone?"

At that moment, a young eagle went soaring by; a beautiful sight for any bird to see, let alone a fellow eagle who knew what it was like to fly with strong wings, and ride the wind as a fearless companion.

"There's no wart on *your* beak, brother eagle, of that I'm sure," said Ebenezer. "I wonder if all eagles find a wart on their beak one day or another? Am I old enough for such a thing to happen to me? No, not at all," he answered himself. "I see eagles older than I am, flying as perfectly as that young one who just went by."

Now that he had said those words, Ebenezer's head drooped lower down still.

"I think it will be best if I sit in a cave somewhere. It will be less embarrassing, for one thing; and perhaps I can study my situation seriously, for another. I'd rather not see any of my friends for a while . . . there would be too much explaining to do. But really . . . how can I explain when I don't even know myself what my trouble is? Yes, for certain, I shouldn't see anyone at all."

So Ebenezer set out to look for the best, most secret cave where he could hide for . . . well, he wasn't quite sure how long.

He walked carefully along craggy paths in his cliff mountain. He had never walked for very long before. His marvelous wings were his favorite way of getting from place to place.

"I must say, this is a different sensation, walking so far. But at least I am learning how other creatures feel who only have legs." Ebenezer kept talking to himself. It seemed to him to be the most helpful thing to do.

"Walking and talking . . . talking and walking . . . be a walking, talking eagle, Ebenezer, for now, anyway."

"Oh dear, but I am really a high-flying, fear-defying eagle! Yes, indeed, that is *really* what I am! I well remember my mother telling me so, as she nudged me out of the nest for the very first time."

"What a fearful sight awaited me that day! The edge of the cliff; the valley so far, far down below; but mother's great wings were above me as she kept moving me to the edge of our mountain home. How I wanted to be back in the soft down of our big nest! How could I know what to expect? A little eaglet who had never flown before?"

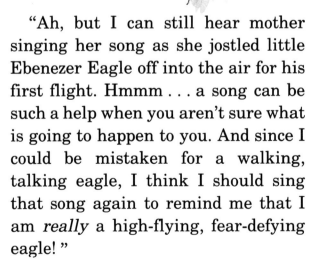

"Ah, but I can still hear mother singing her song as she jostled little Ebenezer Eagle off into the air for his first flight. Hmmm . . . a song can be such a help when you aren't sure what is going to happen to you. And since I could be mistaken for a walking, talking eagle, I think I should sing that song again to remind me that I am *really* a high-flying, fear-defying eagle!"

Then down the craggy pathway, leading down towards the valley, Ebenezer Eagle began to sing the song he had heard so long ago:

"Out of the nest,
   Shoo, shoo, shoo!
Mother knows best
   What eaglets should do!
Don't fear the fall,
   Don't fear the shove;
Trust mother's wings,
   Trust in her love.
         Little wings soon
            Will learn to fly,
         Lifting my eaglet
            Up in the sky.
         High-flying, fear-defying
            Eaglet, that's you!
         Ebenezer Eagle,
            Shoo, shoo, shoo!"

"And I did fly! My wings worked wonderfully well . . . after a few times of practice, and mother catching me."

By now, Ebenezer's legs were getting tired. He had walked quite a long way down the rough mountainside. He was still looking for the perfect cave to hide in. As he rounded a bend, the beautiful sight of a waterfall greeted him.

The waterfall made such pleasant sounds that Ebenezer stopped talking to himself and stood still, to listen to the water instead. He let the water splash on his face; and he even smiled. Then he felt the wart on his beak again, and the smile left.

31

Looking very sad, he perched on a cool rock. And then he saw the cave! It was almost hidden by a big bush and part of the waterfall. It was the perfect place he had been searching for.

With weary legs, Ebenezer crept into the cave. It was cool, and not too dark inside. He was thankful for that, and perched near the entrance, where he could see sunbeams sparkling through the flowing edges of the waterfall. In a little while, he fell asleep.

When he woke up, he was hungry, but he was afraid to leave the cave. As an eagle, he was used to hunting for his meals in the daytime, and sleeping on a safe perch near his great nest.

"Even my daily habits are all mixed up, and I'm more than sure it's this wart on my beak that's upsetting everything about me," mumbled Ebenezer in the heart of the cave.

Then he heard the sound of young boys singing. He trembled as he listened.

"I shouldn't have come down the mountainside this far," he barely whispered. "But then . . . this *is* the perfect cave for me." So he quietly crept to the farthest corner, and forgot about his hunger as he listened to the strange sound of boys' voices so close by. The song wafted into the cave:

32

"They that wait upon the Lord
   Shall renew their strength,
They shall mount up
   With wings as eagles!
They shall run and not be weary,
   They shall walk and not faint,
Mount up, mount up,
   Like the eagle!"

"Eagle! They said, 'eagle'," Ebenezer told himself. He was so happy to hear that word that he stopped trembling.

"Humans can mount up like eagles? I wonder how? Oh yes! They *did* sing, 'They that wait upon The *Lord* shall renew their strength!' "

Then in the softest of whispers he said, "Oh Lord, if humans can find new strength by waiting on You, can You renew *my* strength as I sit here waiting in this cave? Then I could mount up again like eagles; because I *really am* an eagle! Just as You made me."

He could still hear the boys singing, as they faded away in the distance, but Ebenezer sat very still . . . waiting.

After a few moments, he turned his head in the dark corner, and felt a very sharp rock. He rubbed his beak against it; testing it. And just as if a light had shone into his mind, he knew at once what an eagle with a wart on his nose should do.

33

And he knew, too, that such a thought was a high-flying, fear-defying true eagle thought! "Rub the wart against the sharp rock. Grind it off; clean it off; rub, rub, rub until it's gone! Start now, Ebenezer!"

He didn't wait any longer. He started rubbing his beak against the rock. The rock was strong, and Ebenezer was glad of that. Little by little, he could feel the wart wearing down.

Now and again he would stop, step out of the cave and wash in the splashes of the waterfall. Then back to the sharp rock he would go, to keep on cleaning his beak.

Layer by layer, he gradually cleaned away every trace of the troublesome wart. How clean and finely polished his beak felt. Even the sides of his mouth were improved from the polishing.

"I was right to come into this rock cave; I *know* I was right." He felt comforted and thankful.

"I wonder how long I've been here?" By now, he couldn't tell how long he had been in the cave.

After one last washing in the waterfall, he sat in the sun to dry. He loved to face the sun and feel its warmth all over. The sun was shining on his high, cliff home, so he knew it was now morning time.

The new Ebenezer sat up, straight and proud, as eagles should, then looked back at the rock cave.

"Can I mount up again, now, Lord?" he asked eagerly.

And as if in answer, a strong swirling of wind gathered about him. "I can! I know I can!" shouted Ebenezer, with trembling and excitement all mixed together.

The wind grew stronger about him, and with a great cry, Ebenezer rose up on the wind . . . higher and higher. The wart was gone, and so was the clumsiness!

He soared up past his high cliff home; turned on the wind, then sailed down to land on the narrow rock ledge. He landed expertly; a better landing than he had ever done before. His balance was perfect!

Oh, what joy! Back into the air he rose again . . . King of birds, diving faster than any eagle he ever knew! Down through the air he plunged in a dazzling display. As he passed the rock cave he cried out loudly, "Ebenezer Eagle! High-flying, fear-defying! Thank You!" The wind whistled with him as he rose again.

The boys in the valley watched in wonder the glorious flight of Ebenezer Eagle, as he soared off into the sun.

CHOOSING

My little house
　　Has a green front door,
With a latch
　　I can open or lock.
I can say, "Come in!"
　　And open the door,
Or leave it shut
　　When I hear a knock.

My little eyes
　　Have a brown front door,
Which can close
　　Or can open so wide
That I have to watch
　　Which way it will swing,
As I choose
　　What I bring inside!

My little ears
　　Have a pink front door,
I leave open
　　For most of the day;
And so many callers
　　Like to drop in,
With a lot,
　　Or a little to say!

My little mouth
   Has a red front door,
I can open
   Or keep it shut tight.
I can choose what goes
   In and out that door
With a few words,
   Tidy, and polite!

My little heart
   Has a white front door,
With a dear
   Little front door key.
And when Jesus knocked,
   I unlocked it quick!
Now He lives
   There inside with me!

A LETTER TO JESUS

My Very Dearest Jesus,
   It's the ending of the day;
Dad and Mommy kissed me,
   And they listened to me pray.
I'm looking at the stars,
   And they're wide awake like me;
They made me think of You one night
   Beneath an olive tree.
It's hard for me to go asleep,
   So I want You to know
I wish I had been there with You
   Those many years ago.

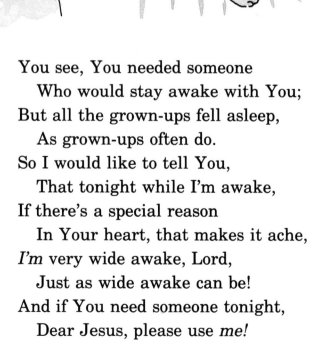

You see, You needed someone
   Who would stay awake with You;
But all the grown-ups fell asleep,
   As grown-ups often do.
So I would like to tell You,
   That tonight while I'm awake,
If there's a special reason
   In Your heart, that makes it ache,
I'm very wide awake, Lord,
   Just as wide awake can be!
And if You need someone tonight,
   Dear Jesus, please use *me!*